HENRY

JAMES

PERCY

MEET ALL THESE FRIENDS IN BUZZ BOOKS:

Thomas the Tank Engine
The Animals of Farthing Wood
Biker Mice from Mars
Winnie-the-Pooh
Fireman Sam
Rupert
Babar

First published in Great Britain 1990 by Buzz Books
an imprint of Reed Children's Books
Michelin House, 81 Fulham Road, London SW3 6RB
and Auckland, Melbourne, Singapore and Toronto
Reprinted 1993 (twice), 1994 (twice), 1995

ISBN 1 85591 000 4

Printed and bound in Italy by Olivotto

THOMAS IN TROUBLE

buzz books

There is a line to a quarry at the end of Thomas's branch line. It goes for some distance along by the road.

Thomas was always very careful there in case anyone was coming.

"Peep, pip, peep!" he whistled, then people got out of the way and he puffed slowly along, with his trucks rumbling behind him.

Early one morning there was a policeman standing close to the line. Thomas liked policemen. He had been a great friend of the Constable who used to live in the village.

"Peep, peep! Good morning!" Thomas whistled.

Thomas expected that this new policeman would be as friendly as the other one. He was sorry to see that the policeman didn't look friendly at all.

The policeman was red in the face and very cross. "Disgraceful!" he spluttered. "I didn't sleep a wink last night – it was *so* quiet."

The policeman looked at Thomas. "And now," he said, "engines come whistling suddenly behind me!"

"I'm sorry, sir," said Thomas. "I only said 'good morning' to you."

"Where is your cow-catcher?" he asked, sharply.

"But, I don't catch cows, sir," said Thomas.

"Don't be funny!" snapped the policeman. He looked at Thomas's wheels. "No side plates, either!" he muttered and he wrote in his notebook.

Then he spoke sternly to Thomas.
"Engines going on public roads must have
their wheels covered and a cow-catcher in
front. You haven't so *you* are dangerous to
the public."

"Rubbish!" said Thomas's driver.
"We've been along here hundreds of times
and there has never been an accident."

"That makes it worse," said the
policeman. And he wrote "REGULAR LAW
BREAKER" in his book.

Thomas's driver climbed back into the cab
and Thomas puffed sadly away.

14

The Fat Controller was having breakfast. He was eating toast and marmalade. His wife had just given him some more coffee.

The butler came in.

"Excuse me, sir," he said. "You are wanted on the telephone."

"Bother that telephone!" said the Fat Controller.

"I am sorry, my dear," he said a few minutes later. "Thomas is in trouble with the police and I must go at once." He gulped down his coffee and hurried from the room.

At the station, Thomas's driver told the Fat Controller what had happened.

"Dangerous to the public indeed! We'll see about that!" said the Fat Controller.

The policeman came onto the platform and the Fat Controller spoke to him at once. But however much the Fat Controller argued with him . . .

. . . it was no good.

"The law is the law," said the policeman, "and we can't change it."

The Fat Controller felt quite exhausted.

"I'm sorry," he said to Thomas's driver. "It's no use arguing with policemen. We will have to make those cow-catcher things for Thomas, I suppose."

"Everyone will laugh, sir," said Thomas, sadly. "They will say that I look like a tram."

The Fat Controller stared at Thomas and then he laughed. "Well done, Thomas! Why didn't I think of it before?" he said.

"We want a tram engine," he went on.
"When I was on my holiday, I met a nice
little engine called Toby. He hasn't enough
work to do and he needs a change. I'll write
to his Controller at once!"

A few days later Toby arrived.

"That's a good engine," said the Fat Controller. "I see that you have brought Henrietta with you."

"You don't mind, do you, sir?" asked Toby, anxiously. "The Station Master wanted to use her as a hen house, and that would never do."

"No, indeed," said the Fat Controller, gravely. "We couldn't allow that!"

Toby made the trucks behave even better than Thomas did.

At first, Thomas was jealous, but he was so pleased when Toby rang his bell and made the policeman jump that they have been firm friends ever since.

THOMAS

EDWARD

GORDON